# Dear Parents:

Congratulations! Your child is taking the first steps on an exciting journey. The destination? Independent reading!

**STEP INTO READING®** will help your child get there. The program offers five steps to reading success. Each step includes fun stories and colorful art or photographs. In addition to original fiction and books with favorite characters, there are Step into Reading Non-Fiction Readers, Phonics Readers and Boxed Sets, Sticker Readers, and Comic Readers—a complete literacy program with something to interest every child.

## Learning to Read, Step by Step!

**Ready to Read   Preschool–Kindergarten**
• big type and easy words • rhyme and rhythm • picture clues
For children who know the alphabet and are eager to begin reading.

**Reading with Help   Preschool–Grade 1**
• basic vocabulary • short sentences • simple stories
For children who recognize familiar words and sound out new words with help.

**Reading on Your Own   Grades 1–3**
• engaging characters • easy-to-follow plots • popular topics
For children who are ready to read on their own.

**Reading Paragraphs   Grades 2–3**
• challenging vocabulary • short paragraphs • exciting stories
For newly independent readers who read simple sentences with confidence.

**Ready for Chapters   Grades 2–4**
• chapters • longer paragraphs • full-color art
For children who want to take the plunge into chapter books but still like colorful pictures.

**STEP INTO READING®** is designed to give every child a successful reading experience. The grade levels are only guides; children will progress through the steps at their own speed, developing confidence in their reading.

Remember, a lifetime love of reading starts with a single step!

*For Andy Sinur,*
*a good soul*

Copyright © 2015 Disney Enterprises, Inc. All rights reserved. Published in the United States by Random House Children's Books, a division of Random House LLC, 1745 Broadway, New York, NY 10019, and in Canada by Random House of Canada Limited, Toronto, Penguin Random House Companies, in conjunction with Disney Enterprises, Inc.

Step into Reading, Random House, and the Random House colophon are registered trademarks of Random House LLC.

Visit us on the Web!
StepIntoReading.com
randomhousekids.com

Educators and librarians, for a variety of teaching tools, visit us at
RHTeachersLibrarians.com

ISBN 978-0-7364-3342-6 (trade) — ISBN 978-0-7364-8222-6 (lib. bdg.)
ISBN 978-0-7364-3343-3 (ebook)

Printed in the United States of America

10 9 8

I am Baymax.

I am a robot.

My best friend is
a boy named Hiro.

DISNEY

BIG HERO 6

# I AM BAYMAX

By Billy Wrecks

Random House 🏠 New York

We fly over the city
of San Fransokyo
and protect its citizens.

I did not always
have armor.
At first I was soft,
white, and squishy!

I was a nurse bot.

My only job was to make

people feel better.

I took care of injuries
and gave big hugs.

Hiro is a genius,
but he was not sure
what to do
with a nurse bot.

Then a masked villain attacked the city.

His name was Yokai.
Hiro knew that we
had to stop him.

When we first fought
Yokai, my soft body
got punched
full of holes.

And I deflated!

Hiro gave me

several upgrades.

# I became an armored crime-fighter!

Now I can fly!

And I am super strong.

Hiro knew we would
need help to fight Yokai.
He fixed up some of
our friends, too!

With his new laser gloves,
Wasabi can cut through
anything!

Honey got a shoulder bag
filled with chemicals she
uses to fight bad guys!

Fred loves comic books
and monster movies.
Now his suit breathes fire
and super bounces!

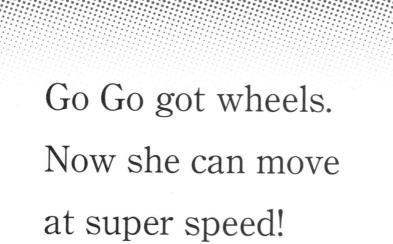

Go Go got wheels.

Now she can move

at super speed!

We became Big Hero 6!
Together, we defeated
Yokai!

We have defended
our city ever since.

No matter what, there is
no challenge too big
for us to face.